Koala Koala

I'm Not A Bear, I'm A Koala.

David G. Earl

Illustrated by T. Kyle Gentry

the Peppertree Press

Sarasota, Florida

For information regarding permission,
call 941-922-2662 or contact us at our website:
www.peppertreepublishing.com or write to:
the Peppertree Press, LLC.
Attention: Publisher
1269 First Street, Suite 7
Sarasota, Florida 34236

ISBN: 978-1-936051-22-9

Library of Congress Number: 2009929160

Printed in the U.S.A.

Printed June 2009

This book is dedicated to my mother Gloria; she is the "G" in David G. Earl. I love you Sweetheart.

—*David G. Earl*

To my nieces Rachel and Nicole. I love you guys. Don't ever forget how unique and special you both are.

—*T. Kyle Gentry*

"You'd better hurry. Wumbatt is waiting for you," Koala Koala's mother pleaded. "And I don't think you've finished your homework."

"We have a new teacher. Today is show and tell and I'm taking my pollywogs!" Koala Koala replied.

Koala Koala and Wumbatt were the first to get to class. They watched everyone push, pull, roll, drag and carry in their show and tells.

Finally, in came the new teacher – through the window.

"I'll get you!" he shouted, chasing a bumble bee into the classroom.

"Hello everyone. I'm Professor Quartz," he proudly announced.

"Today is show and tell! Who'd like to go first?"

A buzz filled the classroom, as everyone sat in silence - no one wanted to go first.

"How about you, little koala bear?" queried Professor Quartz.

Koala Koala looked up at Professor Quartz, who was looking down at Koala Koala.

"Is he talking to you?" whispered Wumbatt.

"You're not a bear are you, Koala? I'm afraid of bears."

"What's your name?" probed Professor Quartz.

"I'm Koala Koala, but everyone just calls me Koala. I'm not a bear, I'm a koala."

11

Professor Quartz was smart, very smart. He knew everything about everything, and he was sure that Koala Koala was a koala bear.

"I have six diplomas and eight degrees!" proclaimed Professor Quartz. "I've studied cats and dogs, lizards and frogs, and I know a koala bear when I see one."

"You have round fuzzy ears like a bear," said Professor Quartz, studying Koala Koala's round fuzzy ears.

"But that doesn't mean that I'm a bear," Koala Koala explained.

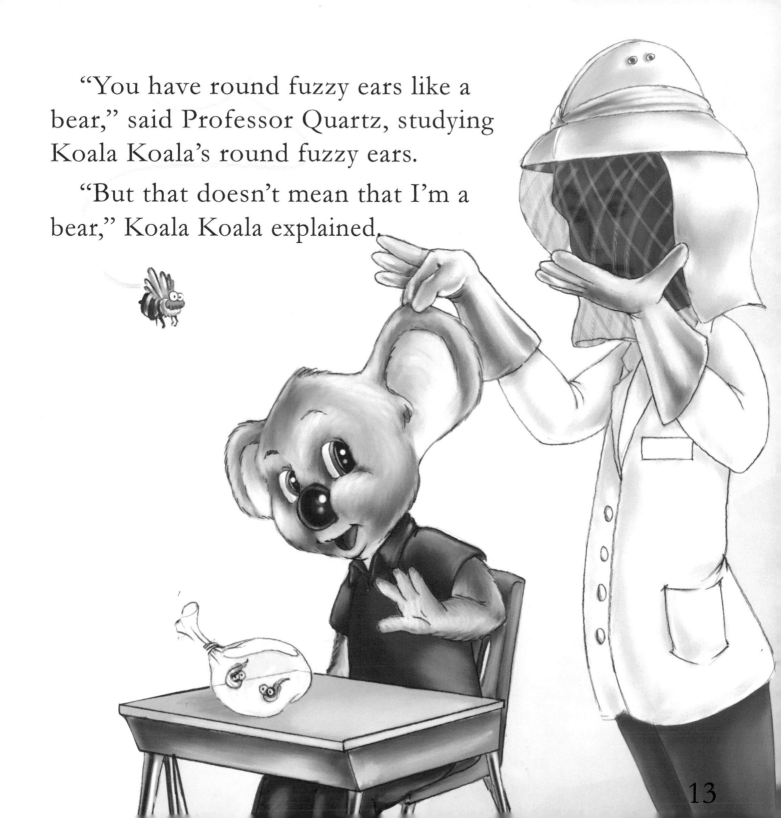

"You have fuzzy fur like a bear," said Professor Quartz, examining Koala Koala's fuzzy fur.

"But I'm not a bear," Koala Koala pleaded.

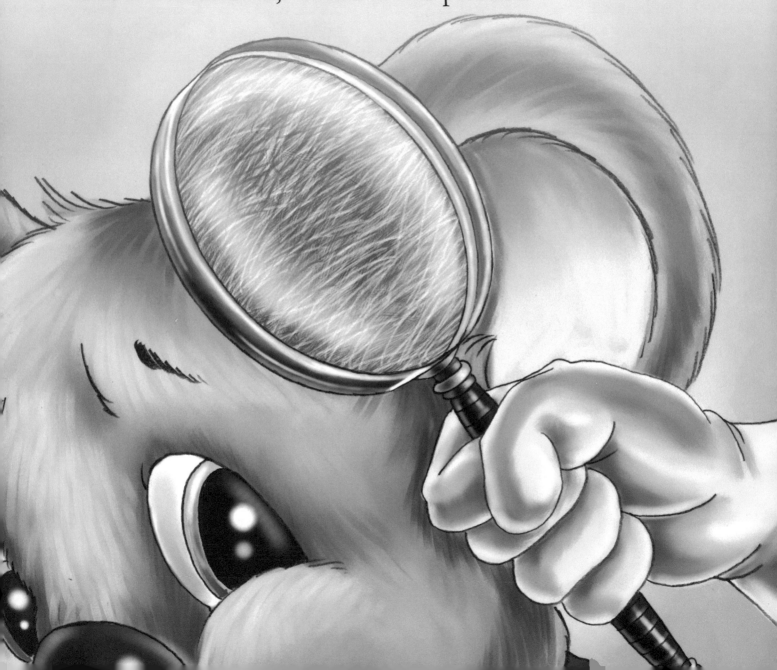

"You even have a cute cuddly face like a bear," said Professor Quartz, observing Koala Koala's cute cuddly face. "Bears have cute cuddly faces, too?" asked Koala Koala.

A loud whisper crept through class as curious eyes tried not to stare.

Even Wumbatt was a little suspicious.

"I'm afraid of bears," Wumbatt whimpered.

When Koala Koala got home, he told his mother and father that Professor Quartz thought he was a bear.

His father told him that koalas are not bears, they are marsupials.

"When you were a baby, you went into my pouch," his mother explained.

"You have a pouch?" asked Koala Koala.

"Yes I do. All marsupial mothers have pouches."

"I'm not a bear! I'm a marsupial!" Koala Koala shouted.

"You are our special little marsupial and we love you very much," said his father.

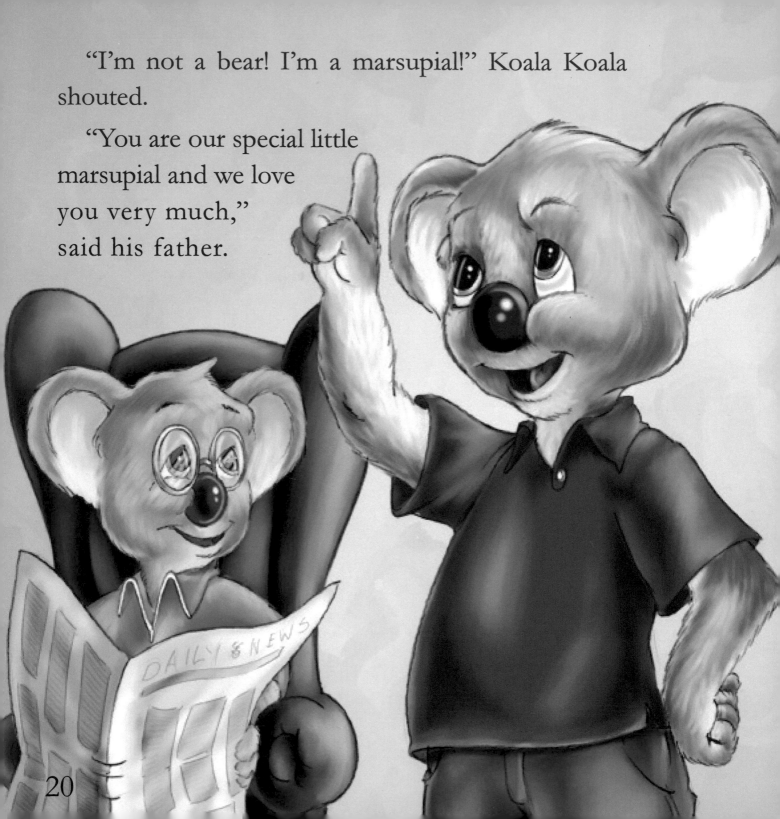

The next morning, Koala Koala was up and dressed before his mother's footsteps reached his door.

He didn't even wait for breakfast.

"I'm not a bear; I'm a marsupial!" Koala Koala repeated to Wumbatt as they hurried to school - bypassing the usual places of interest.

"I'm afraid of bears," muttered Wumbatt.

When Koala Koala and Wumbatt got to school, they found Professor Quartz in the schoolyard — besieged by bees.

23

"I'm not a bear; I'm a marsupial," Koala Koala announced.

"Ohhhh," said Professor Quartz, as nosey ears tried not to eavesdrop.

"When I was born, I went into my mother's pouch."

"Bears are not marsupials are they?" Koala Koala questioned.

"No, they are not," replied Professor Quartz.

"And bears don't have pouches, do they?" Koala Koala inquired.

"No, no they do not," answered Professor Quartz.

"Wellll," said Koala Koala, anticipating a response.

26

Professor Quartz was now confused, so he did what he always did when he was confused - he began to think.

He thought and thought, and thought and thought, and then he thought some more.

"Why do you look like a bear?" asked Professor Quartz.

"I don't look like a bear. Bears look like me."

Suddenly, Professor Quartz realized that he'd made a great discovery!

He discovered that koala bears are not bears at all! They are marsupials.

And that Koala Koala is not a bear; he's a koala, just a koala.

But, Wumbatt was still suspicious.

LaVergne, TN USA
29 September 2009
159372LV00002B

9 781936 051229